HALLOWEEN KITTEN

by Mary Packard
illustrated by Sue Miller

Troll Associates

Tiger was a little kitten who lived with his boy, Joey.

Every night Tiger roamed through the neighborhood, visiting all his friends.

Tiger's first stop was Mrs. Craig's house, where there was always a yummy fish dinner waiting for him.

Next Tiger visited the Peterson home. Their porch light was always on, so there were plenty of moths for the little kitten to catch.

Tiger's last stop was Nutmeg's house. He and his friend liked to play with each other.

Tiger never stayed out very late on his neighborhood walks, though. He always made sure to be home in time to cuddle up in bed with Joey.

But one night, Tiger noticed that things were not quite right. For one thing, all the dogs in the neighborhood were barking.

When he got to Mrs. Craig's house, there was a crowd of strange-looking creatures at her door.

The biggest creature turned around and looked straight at Tiger. It was a lion!

"Meeeowww!" screeched Tiger. He ran off as quickly as he could.

Tiger headed for the Peterson house. But when he got there, the porch light was off. All Tiger saw was a fiery orange face sitting on the porch.

Tiger took off for Nutmeg's house. But Nutmeg was nowhere to be found. Instead, Tiger saw a group of scary monsters standing on the sidewalk.

Tiger's little heart beat faster and faster. He quickly jumped into a tree and hid in the branches until the monsters went away.

As soon as it was safe, Tiger jumped
down from the tree.

But just as he turned the corner near his home,
Tiger ran right into another group of monsters.

MOANNNNNNNOONNNNN

Before he knew it, Tiger was surrounded by the scary creatures. A hairy face with an ugly, green nose peered down at the little kitten. Another creature moaned nearby. And most terrifying of all were the creatures dressed in black wearing pointed hats and cackling!

Suddenly, another figure loomed overhead. Tiger turned to see the lion reaching toward him!

The little kitten arched his back and fluffed up his fur. Then he growled his meanest growl.

GRRRRRGRRRRR

But the lion just laughed. Then he took off his mask.
It was Joey!

Back home they both had
treats and snacks.
Happy Halloween, Tiger!